Dear Parents and Educators,

Welcome to Penguin Young Readers! As parents and educators, you know that each child develops at his or her own pace—in terms of speech, critical thinking, and, of course, reading. Penguin Young Readers recognizes this fact. As a result, each Penguin Young Readers book is assigned a traditional easy-to-read level (1–4) as well as a Guided Reading Level (A–P). Both of these systems will help you choose the right book for your child. Please refer to the back of each book for specific leveling information. Penguin Young Readers features esteemed authors and illustrators, stories about favorite characters, fascinating nonfiction, and more!

Young Cam Jansen and the Lions' Lunch Mystery	LEVEL 3
	GUIDED READING LEVEL J

This book is perfect for a **Transitional Reader** who:
• can read multisyllable and compound words;
• can read words with prefixes and suffixes;
• is able to identify story elements (beginning, middle, end, plot, setting, characters, problem, solution); and
• can understand different points of view.

Here are some **activities** you can do during and after reading this book:
• Character Traits: At the end of the story, Danny describes himself as "silly." Come up with a list of other words to describe him.
• Clues: In this story, Cam used clues to help solve the mystery of Danny's missing lunch. Reread the story and make a list of the clues Cam used to find Danny's lunch.
• Make Connections: Have you ever lost something? What did you do to find it?

Remember, sharing the love of reading with a child is the best gift you can give!

—Bonnie Bader, EdM
  Penguin Young Readers program

*Penguin Young Readers are leveled by independent reviewers applying the standards developed by Irene Fountas and Gay Su Pinnell in *Matching Books to Readers: Using Leveled Books in Guided Reading*, Heinemann, 1999.

For Michelle and Jonathan,
my Dutch cousins—DA

To the Gosselins, John and Liz,
and to the gosling, Zack—SN

Penguin Young Readers
Published by the Penguin Group
Penguin Group (USA) Inc., 375 Hudson Street, New York, New York 10014, USA
Penguin Group (Canada), 90 Eglinton Avenue East, Suite 700, Toronto, Ontario M4P 2Y3, Canada
(a division of Pearson Penguin Canada Inc.)
Penguin Books Ltd., 80 Strand, London WC2R 0RL, England
Penguin Group Ireland, 25 St. Stephen's Green, Dublin 2, Ireland (a division of Penguin Books Ltd.)
Penguin Group (Australia), 250 Camberwell Road, Camberwell, Victoria 3124, Australia
(a division of Pearson Australia Group Pty. Ltd.)
Penguin Books India Pvt. Ltd., 11 Community Centre, Panchsheel Park, New Delhi—110 017, India
Penguin Group (NZ), 67 Apollo Drive, Rosedale, Auckland 0632, New Zealand
(a division of Pearson New Zealand Ltd.)
Penguin Books (South Africa) (Pty.) Ltd., 24 Sturdee Avenue,
Rosebank, Johannesburg 2196, South Africa

Penguin Books Ltd., Registered Offices: 80 Strand, London WC2R 0RL, England

Text copyright © 2007 by David A. Adler. Illustrations copyright © 2007 by Susanna Natti. All rights reserved. First published in 2007 by Viking and in 2008 by Puffin Books, imprints of Penguin Group (USA) Inc. Published in 2012 by Penguin Young Readers, an imprint of Penguin Group (USA) Inc., 345 Hudson Street, New York, New York 10014. Manufactured in China.

The Library of Congress has cataloged the Viking edition under the following Control Number:
2006029076

ISBN 978-0-14-241176-6   10 9 8 7 6

Young Cam Jansen
and the Lions' Lunch Mystery

by David A. Adler
illustrated by Susanna Natti

Penguin Young Readers
An Imprint of Penguin Group (USA) Inc.

Contents

1. Danny's Zoo Riddle..........................5

2. Lunch at the Lions' Den.....................11

3. Lost and Found..............................19

4. Cam Said, "Click!"..........................23

5. A Treat for Everyone......................26

Chapter 1
Danny's Zoo Riddle

"Is everyone here?" Ms. Dee asked.

The children in her class

were in the front of the room.

They were in line getting ready

to visit the zoo.

A few parent helpers were there, too.

Danny got out of line.

"Please," he called out, "help Ms. Dee.

If you're *not* here, raise your hand."

Danny looked at Cam Jansen,
Eric Shelton, and the other children
in Ms. Dee's class.
No one raised his hand.
"Great!" Danny said.
"We're all here.
Now let's go to the zoo."
Beth asked, "If someone is not here,
how can he raise his hand?"
"Get back in line," Ms. Dee told
Danny.

Ms. Dee checked the list of children
in her class.

She looked to see if they were there.

Danny opened a small riddle book.

"Here's a zoo riddle.

What's gray and has 16 wheels?"

Cam Jansen closed her eyes.

She said, "Click!"

Then she told Danny,

"An elephant on roller skates.

That riddle is on page thirty-six."

Cam has an amazing memory.
"My memory is like a camera,"
she says.
"I have pictures in my head
of everything I've seen."
She says *click!* is the sound the
camera in her head makes when
she wants to remember something.
Cam's real name is Jennifer.
But when people found out
about her amazing memory,
they called her "the Camera."

Soon "the Camera" became
just "Cam."
"We're all here," Ms. Dee said.
"Now, please, follow me."
Cam opened her eyes.
She, the other children in her class,
and the parent helpers
followed Ms. Dee outside.
Other classes were already waiting.
Five buses were lined up
by the front curb of the school.

"Take your partner's hand,"
Ms. Dee said.

Cam took Eric's hand.

"Hey," Beth said.

"Where's my partner?

Where's Danny?"

Chapter 2
Lunch at the Lions' Den

"Danny, where are you?"

Ms. Dee shouted.

Danny stuck his head through
an open window on the first bus.

"Here I am," he said.

"Will you please get off that bus,"
Ms. Dee told him.

"Wait here with the class."

Danny got off the bus.

Dr. Prell, the principal, came outside.

She spoke to the children.

"Stay with your group.

Listen to your teachers.

And have a great time at the zoo."

Dr. Prell walked back into the school.

"I hope everyone remembered to bring a bag lunch and to write your name on it," Ms. Dee said.

"When you get on the bus,

drop the bag in the big box.

It's in the front.

Then sit with your partner."

Ms. Dee led her class to the

middle bus.

She stood by the door

as the children got on.

The driver was Mrs. Lane.

A blue box and a yellow box

were in the front of Mrs. Lane's bus.

The blue box was marked
"Lost and Found."
The yellow box was marked
"Lunches."
Cam and Eric dropped their
lunch bags into the yellow box.
They found seats near
the back of the bus.
Danny and Beth sat behind them.

The bus stopped by the front
of the zoo.

Ms. Dee told the children
to stay with their groups.

"We will meet for lunch at noon,"
she said.

"We will meet at the tables
near the lions' den.

I'll bring the lunches."

Cam and Eric got off the bus.

They joined their group.

Mr. Kane, Beth's father,
was their leader.

They went to the monkey house.

Danny pointed at a small monkey.

It was sitting on a swing.

The small monkey pointed
at Danny.

Danny patted his head.

The monkey patted its head.

Danny waved to the monkey.

The monkey waved back.

Next they visited
the black bears and the seals.
Then Mr. Kane said,
"Let's go to the lions' den.
It's time for lunch."
Danny asked, "Is it time for the
lions' lunch?"
"No," Mr. Kane answered.
"It's time for ours."

The yellow box from the bus
was on one of the tables
near the lions' den.
Ms. Dee took the lunches
from the box
and gave them all out.
"Hey!" Danny shouted.
"Where's *my* lunch?"

Chapter 3
Lost and Found

"Is this a joke?" Ms. Dee asked Danny.

"No," he said.

"I had a lunch.

I put it in the box."

"May Cam and I go to the bus to look for Danny's lunch?" Eric asked Ms. Dee.

Ms. Dee looked at Mr. Kane.

"Beth and I will go with them," he said.

"I will, too," Danny said.

They walked through the zoo

to the parking lot.

"My lunch is in a brown bag,"

Danny said as they walked.

"My name is on it."

They walked slowly.

They looked for Danny's lunch.

But they didn't find it.

"There's the bus," Beth said.

Cam, Eric, Beth, and Danny
ran to the bus.

"I lost my lunch," Danny told
Mrs. Lane.

"I dropped it in the box and
now it's gone."

Mrs. Lane put down the mystery
book she was reading.

"Maybe someone dressed up
as Danny and took it."

Mrs. Lane held up her book.

"People wear disguises in this book."

Eric said, "I don't think someone put

on a Danny disguise.

I think Danny put his lunch

in the wrong box.

I think he dropped it in the blue box.

That's the Lost and Found box."

Eric looked through the Lost and

Found box.

He found pencils and mittens,

but he didn't find Danny's lunch.

Chapter 4
Cam Said, "Click!"

"You can have some of my lunch,"

Mrs. Lane said.

She gave Danny an apple

and a small bag of carrot sticks.

Mr. Kane said,

"And I'll buy you a sandwich

and a drink.

Now let's go back to the lions' den."

Eric whispered to Cam,

"But we still don't know

what happened to Danny's lunch."

"Maybe Danny never brought his
lunch," Cam said while they walked.
"Maybe he forgot it at home."
She told Eric to hold her hand.
"I don't want to bump into anyone."

Then Cam closed her eyes
and said, "Click!"
Cam said, "I'm looking at Danny
when we were in the front of
our room.
He had his lunch.
It was in a brown bag."

Cam said, "Click!" again.

"Now I'm looking at Danny when
we were standing outside."

Cam said, "Click!" again.

"That's it!" she said.

She opened her eyes.

Mr. Kane was about to buy
a sandwich and juice for Danny.

"Wait!" Cam called to Mr. Kane.

"I know where to find Danny's lunch."

Chapter 5
A Treat for Everyone

"Danny's lunch is with one of the other classes," Cam said.

"It is?" Danny said.

"Yes," Cam told him.

"You were the first one on the bus this morning."

"Ms. Dee told me to get off, and I did," Danny said.

Cam reminded Danny, "When you got on alone, you got on the first bus.

That's where you left your lunch.

Then our class got on the third bus."

Mr. Kane said, "Danny's lunch must

be with Mr. Tan's class."

Cam, Eric, Danny, Beth, and

Mr. Kane went to the tables where

Mr. Tan's class was sitting.

Danny's lunch was there

in a green box.

Danny stopped at the monkey house.

He waved to the small monkey.

The small monkey jumped up and

down and waved back.

"He likes me," Danny said.

"Of course he does," Mr. Kane

told Danny.

Cam, Eric, Danny, Beth, and

Mr. Kane returned to the lions' den.

Eric told Ms. Dee,

"Cam found Danny's lunch."

He told her how Cam solved

the mystery.

"Great!" Ms. Dee said.

"Cam is lucky to have such a great

memory, and we're lucky she's in

our class.

Now it's time for a treat.

I bought ice cream for everyone."

"Even for me?" Danny asked.

"Yes," Ms. Dee said, "even for you."

"Sometimes I'm silly," Danny said.

Ms. Dee agreed.

"But you're also lots of fun,"
she said.

"I'm glad you're in my class, too."

A Cam Jansen Memory Game

Take another look at the picture on page 31.
Study it.
Blink your eyes and say, "Click!"
Then turn back to this page
and answer these questions:

1. Is Cam Jansen smiling?

2. Are there any birds in the picture?

3. What color are the tables?

4. Is there a banana on one of the
   tables?

5. How many children are sitting and
   eating ice cream?

6. How many lions are in the picture?